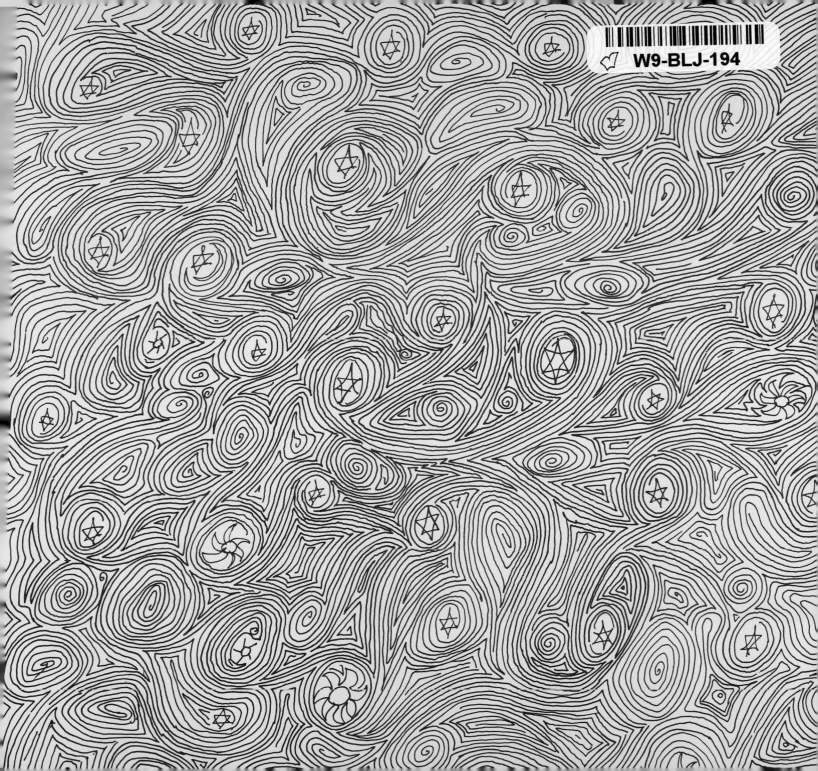

THE RETURN OF THE GOLEM
A Chanukah Story | PETER RUGGILL

Holt, Rinehart and Winston | New York

Library of Congress Cataloging in Publication Data

Ruggill, Peter.   The return of the Golem.

SUMMARY: The Golem, a clay man made by the Rabbi,
saves a small village synagogue from some evil creatures
from outer space.

1. Golem—Juvenile literature. [1. Golem—Fiction.
2. Chanukah (Feasts of Lights)—Fiction] I. Title.

PZ7.R8858Re   [E]   79-4817   ISBN 0-03-053331-7

It was the evening of Chanukah and everyone was in a
rush to get home in time.

Rachel and Benni helped mother prepare for the celebration.

Then they lit the first candle, said a blessing, and sat down to eat.

After dinner father told them the story of Chanukah: how the Greek rulers of Israel dirtied the Hebrew temple and forbade the Hebrew people to practice their religion. The Hebrews organized an army and chased the Greeks away. Then they cleaned the temple and made it holy again. Even though they found enough oil to burn the lamp for only one day, a miracle happened and the oil lasted for eight days. So we celebrate Chanukah for eight days, to remember the struggle for freedom and the miracle of the lamp. The menorah is the symbol, with places for eight candles and one extra standing guard.

Afterward the children played with a dreidel, whose four letters, שׁ ה ג נ, stand for the Chanukah saying "A Great Miracle Happened There."

Before going to bed, Rachel and Benni went out to look
at the stars. They saw a rocket coming down.

It landed in a burst of flame.

Out came some strange-looking creatures. They
behaved peculiarly, then went to the synagogue.

"This," said the Rabbi, "calls for help from the Golem."

He took out a wooden box and removed a shiny lump of clay. Reading from a special book, he began to recite the Hebrew letters: *"aleph, beth, gimmel, daleth..."* As he spoke, each letter jumped up and danced in the air. The letters began to move among themselves and form words.

Suddenly there was a tremendous explosion, and through the smoke a strange form appeared.

There stood the Golem, a giant made of clay who was stronger than an ox. The Rabbi climbed up on the table and drew an *aleph* on its forehead.

"You see," said the Rabbi, "*aleph* is the first letter of the Hebrew word for truth. Only when we are dedicated to the truth are we strong and truly alive." When he finished, the Golem sprang to life.

The Rabbi commanded the Golem to go to the synagogue and chase the creatures away.

The Golem frightened the creatures away and the
rocket blasted off, heading back to space.

Everyone danced around. Then the Rabbi and the children returned to clean up the synagogue.

To their great surprise, they saw that the Golem had gone wild.

"Quick," cried the Rabbi, "climb on my shoulders and erase the *aleph*."

There was a giant explosion in reverse. And the Golem, without an *aleph*, was changed back into a simple lump of clay.

"Sometimes we need force to fight evil," said Rabbi Yosef, "but then force by itself runs wild and becomes evil." They all went home.

"Where have you been?" asked mother when the children returned.

"There was a rocket and spacemen," cried Rachel.

"And Rabbi Yosef made a Golem," Benni added, "and chased them out of the synagogue."

"Oh children, you're lucky I don't give you both a spanking. Chanukah celebrates a victory for the synagogue and a great miracle, but that's no reason to make up stories. Now wash up, say your prayers, and go to bed."

In the evening, on the second night of Chanukah, the children prepared the menorah with two candles, plus one extra standing guard. Rachel and Benni smiled with a secret they both shared. "Happy Chanukah!" they called when the candles were lit.

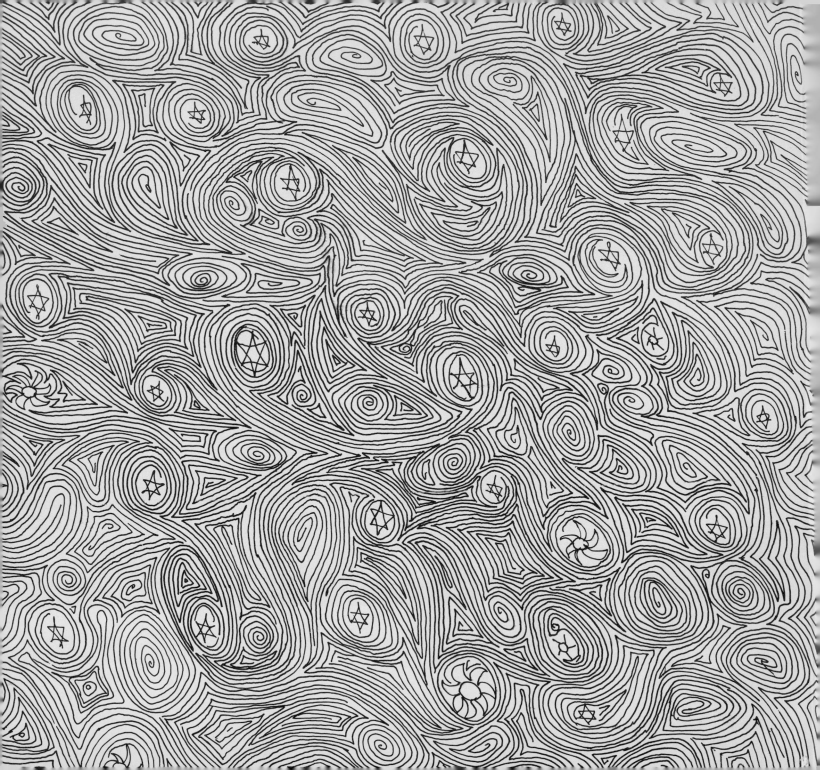